Soon a number of the black-and-white birds gathered around Eliza.

"The volcano is erupting and the lava might reach the cliffs. You have to get into the sea now!" Eliza urged.

"My mommy said to wait until dark to go into the sea," a puffling said.

"That's right! She's right!" the pufflings said in their raspy voices to Eliza.

"Why?" asked Eliza.

"Because there's a gang of mean seagulls out there," growled the puffling. "We're supposed to wait until nighttime, when they might not be around. It's much safer to leave at night. But we're still scared."

"Don't worry," said Eliza. "We'll find a way to help you."

THE WILD THORNBERRYS CHAPTER BOOKS

Race to the Sea

KLASKY
CSUPO, INC.

Based on the TV series *The Wild Thornberrys*® created by Klasky Csupo, Inc.
as seen on Nickelodeon®

ISBN 0-439-36611-9

12 11 10 9 8 7 6 5 4 3 2 1   1 2 3 4 5 6/0

Printed in the U.S.A.

First Scholastic printing, October 2001

Race to the Sea

by Michele Spirn
illustrated by the Thompson Bros.

SCHOLASTIC INC.

New York   Toronto   London   Auckland   Sydney
Mexico City   New Delhi   Hong Kong   Buenos Aires

Chapter 1

"Debbie! Debbie!" Marianne Thornberry called. "Where *is* your sister?" she asked Eliza.

"She's probably in the swimming pool again," Eliza said to her mother.

"Please get her, dear," Marianne said. "We want to go to the cliffs to videotape the puffins."

"Now that the baby puffins are hatched, they must go into the sea soon, Eliza," her father, Nigel, said. "It would be smashing if we could shoot that! Please hurry, poppet."

Eliza grabbed Darwin and ran to the pool formed by an underground hot spring, one of many found in Iceland.

"I don't see her," she said to Darwin.

Eliza started to look around for Debbie when Darwin suddenly clutched her arm.

A lump of gray brown mud with bits of gray stuff all over it rose from the water.

"Eek! A sea monster!" Darwin yelled.

The sea monster opened its mouth. "Hey!" it said. "Why's that chimp going postal?"

"Relax," whispered Eliza to Darwin. "It's Debbie."

Eliza leaned over the edge of the pool. "Maybe he thinks you look like some creepy sea monster, Debbie. What's that junk on your face?"

"I've finally found an awesome mud

pack!" Debbie replied. "It's mud from a volcano, mixed with some Iceland moss. It's the best for zapping zits."

"Mom and Dad are ready to go to the cliffs to videotape the puffins. Come on," Eliza said.

"Why don't you and monkey man there toddle along without me? I'm enjoying this pool too much to leave," Debbie answered.

"You've enjoyed the pool so much that you're starting to look like a prune," Eliza said. "Let's go!"

"Who made you the hall monitor?" Debbie grumbled as she got out of the pool. She examined her hands and feet as she dried herself off.

"Sandpaper skin! If we ever get back to civilization, I'll probably end up looking like an alligator!"

The girls climbed into the Commvee. Darwin grabbed some Cheese Munchies, his favorite snack. Donnie jumped into Eliza's lap.

"Awabbadabba!" shouted Donnie.

"Righty-ho, Donnie," Nigel cheerfully said. "The puffins we see today will be babies called pufflings. They hatched about forty or fifty days ago, and their parents took care of them in the beginning. Now they're on their own."

"But they're only babies!" Eliza protested. "How can they take care of themselves?"

"They're not like human babies," Nigel answered. "They're ready to leave the nest and enter the sea. But they're very poor fliers. Sometimes the children of this island help them by throwing the birds into the sea." Nigel demonstrated by pretending to throw something out of the Commvee window. Donnie laughed and threw a ball at Debbie.

"Ouch! Please stop giving the little pest

ideas!" yelled Debbie as the ball hit her forehead. "Let's get this show on the road."

Just as Nigel revved up the motor, a man ran up to the Commvee. Marianne put her hand on Nigel's arm and cautioned, "Wait."

"Can you help us?" the man asked.

"What's the matter?" Nigel said.

"Eldfell volcano is starting to erupt!" the man explained. "I'm the mayor, and we need as many people as possible to help. Please!"

"Of course," Nigel answered. "But what can we do?"

"We'll work with the firefighters to pour cold water on the lava. Cold lava can't flow. This way we'll try to make sure it doesn't reach the town," the mayor said.

"Sounds exciting!" replied Nigel. "You

can count on me! What do you say, Marianne?"

"I'm right behind you, dear," answered Marianne. "Debbie, I think you're old enough to come along. How about it?"

"No, thanks. I'm going back to that warm pool where I was before Eliza dragged me away," Debbie said.

"Fine," Marianne said, "but you'll have to take your sister and Donnie with you."

"But I don't want to be stuck with the babies!" Debbie protested.

"I'm not a baby!" Eliza exclaimed. "I can take care of myself *and* Donnie *and* Darwin!"

"All right, all right! I'm coming," said Debbie.

"Hurry!" cried the mayor. "There's no time to waste!"

"Eliza," Marianne said, "we'll come back later to check on you."

"They'll be safe," said the mayor. "We've always been able to contain the volcano before. Come! My car's over there."

"Awbada geegeerata," Donnie shouted as Nigel, Marianne, and Debbie went off to the volcano.

"Come on, Donnie," Eliza said in a soothing voice. "We might as well walk down to the cliffs and join the *other* babies—the baby puffins, that is. Maybe they can use our help!"

Chapter 2

As Darwin, Donnie, and Eliza walked to the cliffs, Eliza looked around at the island. "I thought Iceland would be all ice, but it's so green!"

"There's plenty of ice over there," said Darwin with a nod. They looked up from the grassy cliffs to the snow-topped glaciers in the distance.

"But it's *still* warm," Eliza marveled.

"That's because it's summer now," said

Darwin. "But I wouldn't want to be here in the winter."

"I wish we could help at the volcano," Eliza groaned. "I *never* get to do the important stuff." She picked up some stones from the ground and tossed them at the cliffs. Donnie imitated her.

"Stop pouting, Eliza," Darwin urged. "Who wants to be near a volcano? Nasty things! Spitting fire and mud! Much better to be nice and safe and take a walk along the—*oof!*"

An arctic fox ran into Darwin and knocked him to the ground. Then the fox tried to run past Donnie, but he leaped on it and wrestled it to the ground.

"Donnie!" Eliza yelled. "Let it go!"

Eliza pulled him off and bent over the fox. "Are you all right?" she asked.

"You got me," the fox answered. He staggered to his feet. "Tell my wife and kids

I love them! Farewell! Until we meet again in the next world." The fox threw himself down on the ground and rolled around. Then he closed his eyes and lay still.

"Oh, no!" cried Darwin. "I've been attacked by a fox! Help me! Get me an ice pack—or a hot pack! Do something!"

"Oh, Dar, stop being so dramatic!" Eliza waved the Cheese Munchies under Darwin's nose. "Stay here while I get this poor fox some water!" she ordered. She ran back to the Commvee to get some.

Meanwhile Darwin moaned and groaned. "No one jumped on *you*, Eliza. I think I should go back to the Commvee and lie down—with plenty of Cheese Munchies," he whined.

"Globabooda!" shouted Donnie. He pointed to the fox. Darwin whirled around and caught the fox opening an eye. Quickly the fox shut his eye again.

When Eliza came back, Darwin pulled

her over and whispered in her ear. Eliza put the water down and leaned over the fox.

"Well, you fooled me!" she said. "Don't worry. We won't hurt you."

The fox sat up and asked, "How did you know I was all right?"

"Darwin saw you look around when I went to get water," she said. "You're quite an actor, aren't you?"

"Foxes always play dead when we think we're in danger," the fox replied. "I thought your little friend there was going to end up wearing me as a coat."

They watched Donnie as he dug in the ground, throwing dirt all over himself.

"Donnie probably decided you were some new kind of toy or a rug or something," Eliza said. "None of us has ever seen a blue fox before."

"We're always blue in the summer. But you should see us in the winter," the fox said. "We're pure white then, so no one can see us in the snow."

"That's really cool! But where were you going in such a hurry?" Eliza asked.

"It's the volcano! I'm going to get my family and move them away from the lava path," the fox explained. He got up and shook the dirt off himself.

"Where are you going to take them?" Eliza asked.

"I know all the hiding spots on this island," the fox said. "Foxes were here long before any people landed in Iceland."

"But they told us the lava wouldn't come this far," Eliza said. She looked at the cliffs where the baby puffins nested.

"Well, it's better to be safe than sorry," the fox warned. "There's always a chance that the hot lava might reach town. If I were one of those birds, I'd get out of here and into the water in a hurry!"

Chapter 3

"Do you think the puffins know about the volcano?" Eliza asked the fox.

"Hmm . . . maybe not," the fox said. "They stay in their holes most of the time." The fox looked up at the sun. "I've got to go," he said. "Nice meeting you." He ran off before Eliza could say good-bye.

Eliza turned to Darwin. "I think we'd better tell the puffins about the volcano."

Eliza, Darwin, and Donnie ran to the

cliffs. At the edge they stared down at hundreds of little holes dug in the side of the cliffs.

"These cliffs are so full of holes, they look like Swiss cheese," Darwin remarked.

"Those little holes must be where the baby puffins live," Eliza said.

"It looks like there are thousands of them," said Darwin.

"Mom said that ten million pufflings are hatched each year in Iceland," said Eliza.

"That's a lot of birds to talk to," Darwin said. "Eliza, how are you going to do that?"

"I'm just going to try to find a leader," declared Eliza. "Someone who can organize them."

She scrambled down the side of the cliff with Darwin and Donnie close behind her. Birds peeked out to see who was coming. When they saw Eliza and the others, they ran deep into their holes.

"Uh-oh! I think we're scaring them," Darwin said.

"We're here to help you!" Eliza cried.

Slowly one puffling poked the tip of her yellow, red, and blue-gray bill out of a hole.

"Go away, big things!" she growled.

"But you can't stay here!" Eliza warned. "Did you know that the volcano is erupting?"

The bird came out of her nest and ran into another nest. Soon a number of the black-and-white birds gathered around Eliza.

"The volcano is erupting and the lava might reach the cliffs. You have to get into the sea now!" Eliza urged.

"My mommy said to wait until dark to go into the sea," a puffling said.

"That's right! She's right!" the pufflings

said in their raspy voices to Eliza.

"Why?" asked Eliza.

"Because there's a gang of mean seagulls out there," growled the puffling. "We're supposed to wait until nighttime, when they might not be around. It's much safer to leave at night. But we're still scared."

"Don't worry," said Eliza. "We'll find a way to help you."

"Oh, dear," sighed Darwin. "I knew *that* was coming!"

Chapter 4

Meanwhile, at the base of the volcano, the other Thornberrys were working hard as the volcano erupted and lava flowed toward town.

"Watch out for the water, Debbie!" cried Marianne.

"Outstanding, Marianne!" shouted Nigel. "I just wish we had brought the video cam to tape this."

The dull red lava still flowed. Debbie

and Nigel filled more buckets with water and passed them along to others who were throwing the water onto the fiery stream of lava.

Marianne straightened up and rubbed her back. "Wow, am I sore!" she said.

"Why don't you take a break?" suggested the chief firefighter. "We've got enough people here now so that you can take a rest."

"I'd like to go and check on my younger daughter," said Marianne. "We left her back where we're camped."

"That's a good idea! In the next two hours, we'll know if the lava will reach town. Then you can move her if you need to," the firefighter said.

"Wonderful!" exclaimed Nigel, rubbing his hands together. "Now we can get the camera, and my wife can videotape the action. It'll make for quite a dramatic piece on our next show."

The Thornberrys got a ride with one of the women going back to town.

"I can't believe there are hot springs everywhere and I'm so grubby," Debbie said. "I need some serious soaking time!" She brushed her hair back with a hand that was black with soot.

"I don't think any of us would win prizes for cleanliness," said Marianne. All of them were covered with ashes and streaks of dirt.

At the Commvee, Marianne ran in to check on Eliza.

"Nigel, they're not here!" Marianne shouted.

"Relax, pumpkin. They couldn't have gone far," Nigel said. "I'll just grab a kipper or two, and then I'll look for them."

"I wonder if they went to the cliffs," Marianne said.

"I'll go look, Marianne," Nigel said.

"Perhaps our Eliza has discovered the pufflings. I must say I'd like to get a look at the little creatures. That would be getting two birds with one stone!" he said with a laugh.

"Nigel, find Eliza and the others *first*, and worry about the birds *second*," said Marianne.

"Of course, love," Nigel said.

When he reached the cliffs, he stopped for a moment to look at the pufflings in their nests. Then he called, "Eliza! Eliza! Where are you?"

"Dad!" Eliza cried. "We're here." She climbed up to meet him, and Donnie and Darwin followed her.

"Eliza! Good, you're all safe!" Nigel said, smiling. "Your mother and I were worried about you."

"Sorry, Dad, but the pufflings need our help to get past the seagulls," Eliza said.

"Poppet," said Nigel, "please stay close by the Commvee so we can find you. This really is a dangerous situation, and we don't want you wandering about."

"But, Dad, I need to be here to heɪp the pufflings. If the lava comes this way, they'll be trapped," Eliza explained.

"Eliza," said Nigel, "don't you understand that if the lava comes this way we'll have to leave as fast as cheetahs?"

"Oh, Dad, can't I just try for a little while? These poor little birds are so helpless," Eliza pleaded.

Nigel looked at his watch and said, "I'll give you two hours. No more than that, Eliza. Then I insist that you go back to the Commvee for safety's sake!"

"Thanks, Dad!" cried Eliza, throwing her arms around Nigel and hugging him.

"Just be careful, Eliza," warned Nigel. "I don't know what you can do in two hours. I wish I could stay with you, but I'm needed at the volcano. Ta, ta, love, and remember, be back at the Commvee in two hours—no later!"

Chapter 5

"Oh, Dar, we don't have much time," said Eliza. "Let's find out if the pufflings are ready to go."

"Pufflings? Go? I think not, Eliza," Darwin said. "There's danger. We have to leave immediately!"

"Dad said we have two hours," Eliza replied. "I intend to use every minute. Are you with me or what?"

"Oh, very well," grumbled Darwin. "But

if I see even one little piece of burning rock, it's back to the Commvee, pronto!"

They climbed down the cliffs again and stood near one of the nests.

"Hello!" called Eliza.

"Who's there?" a puffling called back.

"It's me, Eliza," she answered.

"It's that big thing again," said one puffling to another.

"Are you ready to go into the water?" Eliza asked.

"We told you before that we can't leave until the seagulls go away," a puffling said. "We have to wait until the coast is clear."

"But the lava could be here in two hours! Then you'll *really* be trapped," Eliza said.

"But we can't figure out anything to do but wait," said the puffling. "Unless, maybe, you can help us?"

"Think, Darwin. How can we help

them? We only have two hours," Eliza said urgently.

"What can *we* do?" asked Darwin. "We need to find a safe place for ourselves! I know. We can go back to the Commvee, put our feet up, and relax with some Cheese Munchies."

"Darwin! How can you be so selfish! The pufflings are in danger! They're just babies," said Eliza. "They don't know any better."

"Well, really, Eliza, I don't know what you want me to do," said Darwin.

"I guess the only thing left is to talk to the gulls," Eliza said.

"Not me! Oh, no! They've got sharp little beaks, those fellows. I've seen them," Darwin said.

"Darwin! Please," begged Eliza. "Don't worry. I'll protect you."

"And what can you do against those flying machines? I tell you those gulls can be rough when they want to," said Darwin. Eliza turned away from Darwin. "Okay. I'll go myself," she announced. "Fine, I'll go. But I'm going under protest. Remember that," said Darwin. "Wait for me!"

"I'd better check on Donnie first," Eliza said. "Donnie! Donnie!" she called. Then she heard a strange cackling sound. She looked down and spotted Donnie turning a somersault surrounded by a group of pufflings.

"Donnie, we have to go," Eliza said.

"Oh, please let him stay," said one of the pufflings. "He's very funny."

"All right, I'll be back for him soon," Eliza said.

"No hurry," said the puffling.

Eliza and Darwin scrambled down to the seashore.

"Squawk! Strangers coming! Squawk!

Maybe they have something to eat!" the leader of the seagulls called to the others.

"Please come closer," Eliza said.

"Why?" squawked the leader.

"I want to talk to you," Eliza replied.

"And I want to squawk at you," said the gull. His friends roared with laughter.

"I told you they wouldn't listen," said Darwin nervously.

"What's old furry there saying?" asked the leader. "I can't hear you. Maybe if I get a little closer . . ."

With a mighty flap of his wings, the seagull zoomed in close to Darwin and buzzed around his head. Darwin buried his head in his hands.

"He's shaking! You're scaring him!" shouted Eliza. "Stop it!"

"This is our turf," said the seagull. "Go back up the cliffs where you belong and leave us alone! Or you'll be sorry."

Chapter 6

The gull flew back to his friends in the ocean.

"Whew! Those pufflings weren't kidding about the gulls," Eliza said.

"What did I tell you?" exclaimed Darwin. "But no, you wouldn't listen to me! You *had* to talk to the seagulls yourself. Now let's go back to the Commvee!"

"There must be a way to get them to move," Eliza said.

"Eliza! Didn't you see him threaten to attack me?" Darwin asked.

"Didn't you hear what they said when we were walking toward them?" she asked.

"Don't ask me," said Darwin. "I was too busy trying not to have my fur pecked off."

"They said they were hungry!" Eliza exclaimed.

"Hungry for what?" Darwin asked. Then he clutched his bag of Cheese Munchies as he saw where Eliza was looking.

"No, sirree! I'm not giving up my Cheese Munchies to some barbaric gulls," he insisted. "There are hardly any left."

"How many are there?" Eliza asked.

"Not telling," Darwin said, trying to hide the bag behind his back.

"Come on, Darwin," Eliza pleaded. "We

don't have much time left. It's going to be dark soon. Then we'll have real problems getting the pufflings into the water."

"All right. If you must know, there's half a bag left," Darwin said, looking in the bag.

"That might work," said Eliza. "Here's what I want you to do." She whispered her plan to Darwin, who tried to resist. Finally, he gave in.

Darwin walked slowly down to the shore. He opened the bag of Cheese Munchies. The seagulls stared at it. Eliza could hear them talking.

"What's he got there?" asked one.

"It sure smells good," said another.

Then Darwin slowly took out a Cheese Munchie and dropped a piece of it on the beach. He turned away. In a flash the seagull leader flew over to it, picked it up in his beak, and flew back to the others.

"It's salty," he reported. "Tastes good. I think it's something to eat."

Darwin started walking back to the Commvee. Every few yards, he would drop a piece of a Cheese Munchie behind him. As Eliza had hoped, the hungry seagulls followed him.

Meanwhile, she ran up to the puffling holes.

"Quick! The seagulls are gone," she said. "You can get into the water now."

"Where did they go?" the pufflings asked.

"My friend Darwin is distracting them for a while," she said. "Are you ready?"

"Are you sure it's safe?" they asked.

"Yes, it's safe now," declared Eliza.

It took the pufflings a while to waddle out of their holes and climb up the cliffs. Donnie came last.

"What's taking you so long?" Eliza asked the pufflings.

"We have to line up just right," one answered.

"Let me help," said Eliza. "Here, come this way." She directed the pufflings to the perfect spot.

Finally, all the birds were lined up on the cliff.

"Please hurry!" she cried. "I don't want you to be trapped by the lava!"

"We're ready!" rasped a puffling. "Make sure the coast is clear!"

Eliza looked around and over the cliffs.

"Cleared for takeoff!" she shouted.

Racing down the cliffs, the first puffling flapped its wings and left the ground. Up in the air it flew. It flapped its wings very fast. It was getting dark and Eliza could hardly see. But she heard the puffling splash into the water.

"Hooray! He made it!" she cried. "Come on! Let's go!" She helped the other pufflings take their turns.

Each time they heard a splash, Donnie

laughed and clapped. Many splashes later Eliza turned around. "Whew! They made it in time," she said with relief.

Suddenly she realized she was seeing white spots on the road. Some pufflings had lost their way. Now they were headed toward town!

Chapter 7

"Come on, Donnie!" Eliza called. "We have to catch the birds before they end up in town."

Eliza put him on her shoulders and raced to head off the pufflings.

"Stop! Stop! You're going the wrong way!" she shouted.

"Isn't that water?" asked one puffling. "That looks like water ahead." The puffling stared at the lights of town.

"No way," said Eliza. "The water's over here!"

The pufflings turned in a circle. They started to follow Eliza, but some got confused and turned the other way.

Eliza ran back and forth trying to turn the stray pufflings in the right direction. But the baby birds were getting more and more mixed up and tired.

"We're trapped!" cried the pufflings. They started flapping their wings wildly. But they couldn't fly at all.

"You're not trapped," said Eliza. "I'll get you back to the ocean."

"But we can't fly from flat ground," rasped a puffling. The pufflings gathered in a group and started to growl.

"Arr! Arr!" they cried. "We'll never get back. We want our mommies!"

"Quick! Let's hurry back to the cliffs," said Eliza. "Time is running out!"

Eliza began to herd the scared pufflings back to the cliff.

"Come on," she urged them. "You can do it."

Finally, they reached the cliffs.

"I'm too tired to flap my wings," a puffling growled. "How will I ever get into the water?"

Eliza looked down at the ocean. It was a long drop. Then before she could stop him, Donnie grabbed a puffling and threw it over the cliff.

"Donnie! What are you doing?" she yelled. Donnie pointed to the ocean. Eliza heard the splash of the bird landing safely.

"Throw me! Throw me!" the pufflings cried. "If you throw us, we can get the speed we need. We'll land in the water safely too."

"Hey! Why didn't I remember what Dad said about throwing the birds!" Eliza exclaimed, smiling.

She grabbed a puffling and threw it over the cliff.

"Thank you!" the puffling yelled as it soared in the air.

She and Donnie threw bird after bird. Finally, all the birds had gone.

"Well, Donnie, we did it," sighed Eliza. "Let's go back to the Commvee. We can just make it!"

As they ran back, they heard a terrible racket.

"That's coming from the Commvee!" Eliza exclaimed. "I hope Darwin's okay!" She and Donnie raced faster.

Inside the Commvee they saw Darwin trying to sweep. He kept knocking the broom into things. There was a pile of flour on the floor. Pictures dangled from the walls. Debbie's clothes were flung around and Marianne's favorite bowl was in pieces.

"Darwin, what's going on?" Eliza asked.

"You finally came back! Look at this mess! I can't even begin to clean it up!" he cried.

"What happened?" Eliza asked.

"It was those nasty seagulls you insisted I bring back here. They ate all the Cheese Munchies! And they got mad when there were none left. So they made a mess and took off," he said wearily.

"I'm sorry," Eliza said. "But we did get all the pufflings into the sea." She took the broom from Darwin and began to clean up.

Marianne, Nigel, and Debbie came into the Commvee.

"Mom! Dad! What happened with the volcano?" Eliza asked.

"We stopped the lava," Marianne said, yawning.

"I have to admit, it was totally cool," said Debbie.

"It was ripping!" Nigel exclaimed. "Your mother got some lovely shots, too." Then he stepped in flour, looked down at his shoes, and said, "Eliza? What's all this?"

"My clothes!" yelled Debbie. "You trashed them!"

"Look at this place, Eliza!" Marianne exclaimed. "What happened?"

"I'm sorry, Mom, but I had to. We needed to distract the seagulls so the pufflings could get into the water. I didn't know they would make such a mess. But I'll clean it up!"

"It's all right, honey, it sounds like you did it for a good cause."

"What a day!" exclaimed Nigel. "We stopped the lava—"

"I shot some wonderful footage," Marianne said.

"And Darwin, Donnie, and I helped the pufflings," Eliza added.

"Let's help Eliza clean up," said Marianne.

"Like I don't have better things to do than help birdbrain here," snorted Debbie.

"The sooner we clean up, the sooner you can go back to your nice pool," said Nigel.

Debbie grabbed the broom from Eliza and smiled. "Just another typical day in the Thornberry family zoo!"

Discovery Facts

Arctic Fox: The Arctic fox lives in cold regions of the world such as Northern Canada, Alaska, and Iceland. Foxes are the oldest animal life in Iceland.

Iceland: Iceland is a country in Europe about the size of Kentucky. It was discovered by Vikings more than one thousand years ago. There are approximately 275,000 people living there.

Iceland Moss: Iceland moss grows on the plains and hardened lava slopes. It can be used as food or in soap and face cream.

Puffins: Puffins are about a foot long with white bodies and black wings. Atlantic puffins, which live in Iceland, have yellow, bluish gray, and red bills. Puffins have webbed feet for the water and only come ashore to have babies.

Pufflings: Baby puffins, called pufflings, leave the nest as soon as their wing feathers have fully grown. In Heimaey (HAY-mah-ay), Iceland, children gather pufflings that go the wrong way and throw them off the cliffs into the ocean. Pufflings make "growling" sounds to communicate.

Seagulls: Seagulls have long wings, webbed feet, and are white and gray. Seagulls are the enemies of puffins and will attack them.

Volcanoes: Iceland has seventy volcanoes, vents or holes in the earth, that have erupted during the last ten thousand years. In 1973, when Eldfell volcano erupted, hot lava covered a third of Heimaey. The Icelanders sprayed water on the lava to harden it so it would form a dam against new lava.

About the Author

Michele Spirn has written more than fifty books and more than seventy video scripts and filmstrips for adults and children. Among her works for children are a retelling of *The Nutcracker,* the beginning reader series *The Know-Nothings,* a biography of Olympic athlete Jackie Joyner-Kersee, and *All Washed Up,* an 8 x 8 paperback featuring The Wild Thornberrys. She teaches creative writing at New School University in Manhattan, and lives in Brooklyn, New York, with her family.